Spelling Time

Activity Workbook

This book belongs to

....

....

Wonder House

Beginning Vowel Sounds

The alphabets a, e, i, o and u in the English language are known as vowels. A vowel sound is made with an open vocal tract, which includes the lips, throat, tongue, and nose.

Here are a few examples of words that begin with a vowel sound.

ant

elephant

igloo

orange

umbrella

The following words begin with a vowel sound. Help Pebbles the parrot fill in the missing letters. Utter each word aloud as you write.

_pple

_ce cream

_wl

_agle

_ctopus

_ncle

_gg

_nkpot

Can you help Dany the dog to circle the letter that matches the beginning vowel sound of the given pictures?

a	e	i	o	u

a	e	i	o	u

a	e	i	o	u

a	e	i	o	u

a	e	i	o	u

a	e	i	o	u

Each of these words is missing the first letter.
Help Spidy the spider complete the crossword
by filling in the right vowel.

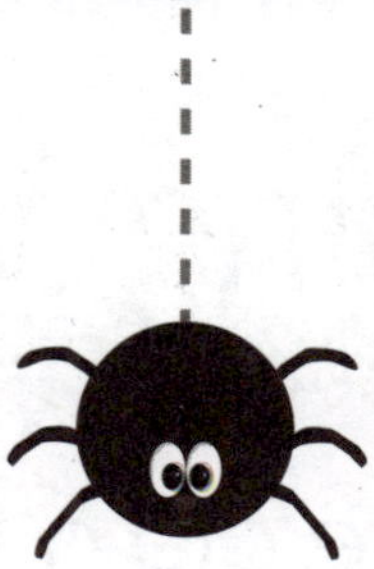

	n	g	e	l
c				
o				
r				
n				

	a	g	l	e
l				
f				

	s	l	a	n	d
c					
e					

	c	e	a	n
t				
t				
e				
r				

	n	d	e	r
n				
c				
l				
e				

	n	s	e	c	t
r					
o					
n					

Ending Vowel Sounds

Here are a few examples of words that end with a vowel sound

gorilla

cycle

sushi

tomato

emu

The following words end with a vowel sound. Help Molly the mouse fill in the missing letters. Utter each word aloud as you write.

t i s s u _

t a x _

p i a n _

m e n _

k i w _

m a n g _

p i z z _

Help Chirpy bird to find and circle the words that ends in a,e,i,o and u.

tomato rainbow

idea sun frill kettle media cup

volcano soup pen banana bottle

emu lake you theater bonsai piano

ski tea plateau dice litchi

video plain

Now, write the words you found. Read aloud each word.

-a	-e	-i	-o	-u

Say what you see in the pictures and listen to its ending sound. Then write the letter that makes the sound. Now, color the pictures.

tax_

glob_

tornad_

moustach_

sk_

lav_

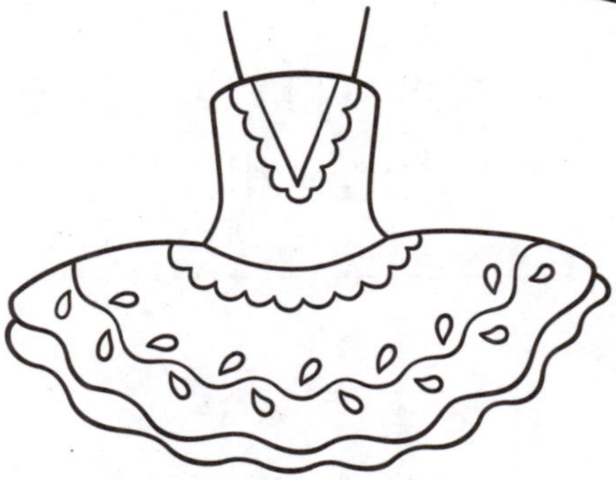

tut_

Middle Vowel Sounds

Let's look at a few examples of words that have a, e, i, o and u in the middle. Read each word aloud.

cup

bag

pen

box

tin

mop

bus

pin

den

tap

Can you write 5 more words with a vowel in the middle?
Say the words out loud as you write.

Fill in the missing middle letter from the table and complete the sentences.

a	e	i	o	u

1. Martha was sitting on a l _ g. 

2. Rony has a blue b _ b. 

3. The s _ n rises in the east and sets in the west. 

4. Andy put on his c _ p to go out. 

5. The boy captured the bird with a n _ t. 

6. The fly is trapped in a spider w _ b. 

7. Throw the paper in a recycle b _ n. 

8. School picnic is so much f _ n. 

Read aloud the words given in the grid. Circle the objects that you spot in the picture.

sun	tin	top	bin	web	dog
fan	man	fig	box	keg	cap
boy	tub	cat	log	den	toy

Fill in the missing letters of the words and complete the sentences.

nib	**bug**	**fox**
put	**leg**	**dam**

1. I live near a _ _ m.

2. P _ _ the pencil in the box.

3. A _ _ x is a clever animal.

4. Diana broke her l _ g.

5. Shina has a gold _ _ b fountain pen.

6. A b _ _ crawled over Elly's arm.

Consonants

All the letters in the alphabet apart from the vowels a, e, i, o and u are known as consonants. A consonant represents a sound produced by blocking the breath in the vocal tract.

There are 21 consonants. Here are a few examples of words beginning with a consonant sound.

cow	parrot	tube	sparkle
zebra	hockey	yacht	nest
	queen	kite	

Now, circle the words that begin with a consonant sound.

toucan panda under carrot

mango tiger otter

orange igloo eagle sky

donkey tomato ice cream

ape umbrella gorilla spoon

love ink pot airplane

Look at the pictures and fill in the missing consonants to complete each word.

_ o o t _ a _ _

f _ o _ e _

_ r e _ s

c _ e _ r _

_ e a _

_ t a _

Beginning Consonants

Look at each picture and complete the words. Now, circle the picture that does not start with the given consonant. Read aloud each word as you write.

Z

_ e _ _ a

_ i _

D

_ _ o o _

_ a _

P

_ a _ _ a

_ e _ t

m

_ a _ _ o

_ e _ _

F

_ e e

_ i _ h

Choose the correct pair of beginning and ending consonants and complete the word. Molly is here to help you!

_ i s _

f,h	t,h	f,g

_ e m o _

c,e	l,n	d,n

_ l a n e _

b,t	c,y	p,t

_ i g e _

g,p	t,r	b,t

_ c a r _

s,f	s,p	n,y

Double Letters

Some words have double letters like **zz, ss, ff, ll, ee and oo**. These could come in the end or in the middle. Such words make a single sound.

Molly the mouse is here to give you examples of some words.

shell	daffodil	cheese	igloo
bull	puzzle	tree	toss
	zoo	buzz	

Can you think of some other words? Say each word aloud as you write.

If a word consists of a single vowel and the word ends in consonant f, l, s or z then double the last letter.

Can you complete the words by adding the double letters?

sleep	**buzz**	**free**	**teeth**	**pull**
dress	**pizza**	**muff**	**glass**	**staff**

1. Anna broke the gla _ _ window.

2. Richard goes to office in a sta _ _ bus.

3. Anita has a beautiful red dre _ _.

4. Peter likes to eat pi _ _ a.

5. Amanda and Joey set their pet dog fr _ _.

6. Bats don't sl _ _ p at night.

7. A monster has big t _ _ t h.

8. Rick asked Mady to pu _ _ a chair for him.

9. Ira has bought a white fir mu _ _.

10. The bees bu _ _.

Sort the words

Read the clues on the corresponding page and find the double letter words that are hidden in the grid. Write the words in the space next to each clue.

C	U	F	F	S	G	N	I	G	G	I	D
I	I	J	A	Y	P	D	U	C	L	I	N
T	U	D	H	T	U	L	I	P	E	O	O
E	T	V	S	H	E	L	L	E	B	W	I
S	L	I	V	B	I	A	R	S	N	Q	S
E	U	H	E	U	E	T	A	S	S	D	M
V	N	C	N	O	O	N	S	K	S	Y	U
D	G	L	A	S	S	E	S	S	A	N	F
A	H	A	Z	K	U	M	L	S	R	A	F
I	Q	Z	P	L	A	E	A	A	G	S	I
D	A	Y	C	S	J	N	B	L	P	T	N
J	U	W	O	O	L	T	A	M	E	Y	C

1. You wear these when your eye sight is weak ....

2. Found on beaches and sea shores ....

3. Opposite of short ....

4. A plant grows up to become this ....

5. End part of a sleeve that has buttons over it ....

6. 12 'o clock during day ....

7. All cows eat this ....

8. A kind of music genre originated in USA ....

9. Sweaters are knitted of this material ....

10. A cupcake is also called ....

Sound Blends

Sound blends are a set of two or three consonant letters that when pronounced together, retain their sound. Blends are found either at the beginning or end of a word. Dany has a list of some blends for you to understand.

br
- break
- brown
- brand
- brick

ng
- wing
- king
- bang
- long

st
- star
- stand
- stem
- stop

sn
- snake
- snack
- snow
- snore

sp
- spin
- spy
- spray
- spoil

gr
- graph
- grow
- gram
- grapes

gl
- glow
- glove
- glue
- glass

scr
- script
- scrub
- scream
- screw

fr
- frame
- fresh
- friend
- fry

dr
- drop
- drive
- dress
- draw

nk
- chunk
- thank
- blink
- honk

Look at the pictures and fill in the missing blends. Chirpy bird is here to help you.

The _ _ og came out of the water.

Amy deposited the cheque in the ba _ _.

_ _ ink one glass of milk everyday.

_ _ ush your teeth daily.

He was born with a silver _ _ oon in his mouth.

A model of the earth is called a _ _ obe.

Match the blends in the left column to the letters in the right to complete each word.

st	ider
sn	um
sp	ipt
gr	ail
gl	ork
scr	oves
fr	own
dr	ass
br	uit

Can you fill in the missing sound blends in the story?

Long, lo _ _ ago, there lived a big _ _ ider on a tree.

One day he _ _otted a _ _ ake _ _ iding through the

_ _ ass. Spider _ _ _ eamed and _ _ opped its prey. The

spider got _ _ ightened and was ready to cry. His dear

_ _ iend, _ _ og pacified him. He said, the _ _ ake has

come to meet him and will not harm any one.

Magical e

Molly is adding the letter **e** to his words.
Can you help him?

Now, read aloud and listen how each word changes.

tap_
↓
……………………

kit_
↓
……………………

rob_
↓
……………………

cub_
↓
……………………

hop_
↓
……………………

mat_
↓
……………………

pin_
↓
……………………

cut_
↓
……………………

not_
↓
……………………
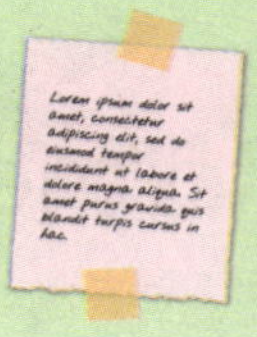

Help Froggy identify each picture. Then, write the word and add **e** to make a new word.

.... + e = ...

.... + e = ...

.... + e = ...

.... + e = ...

.... + e = ...

Same sound, different spellings

Some sounds can be spelled in more than one way. Chirpy has made a list of some words with different spellings.

tray, trait

wait, weight

sister, system

saw, sour

Choose the right spellings for each.

ay or ai	oi or oy
t _ _ l	b _ _ l
r _ _ n	_ _ l
d _ _	t _ _
s n _ _ l	e n j _ _
h _ _	c _ _ n
v _ _n	n _ _ s e

i and y words

Could you help Dany choose
i or **y** to complete the words?

w r _ t e r	f r _	p r _ m e
t _ p e	m _ l d	g _ m
s _ n k	d o l p h _ n	f _ n a l

Now, circle the words that are spelled correctly and write them below.

rhythm	ginger	pyramid	rithm
bicicle	piramid	bicycle	gynger

....

....

....

Rhyming Words

Best and Test both have same sound. Words that rhyme have same ending sounds.

Can you think of some words that rhyme with 'rain' and 'door'?

Can you help Dany match the pictures with the words that rhyme? Say the words out loud.

coat

toad

tree

sock

top

feel

blue

pail

dig

rack

Read the sentences and write the word that rhymes with the word in red.

The pot is h _ t.

There is a mouse in the _ ou _ _.

My coat is in the b _ _ t.

The frog jumped over the _ o _ .

The king likes to s _ n _ .

Keep the fish in the _ i s _.

Arya likes to bake a _ a _ e .

The hen walked into the lion's _ en.

Rita wants to sell her golden b _ l _.

The man is sitting in the v _ n .

Read the rhyme and fill in the missing letters. Take help from the word bank.

mat	**play**	**asleep**	**do**

CAT ON A MAT

Nim the cat was round and fat
He slept all day on a blue _a_.

Ardy the rat said, 'Hey, let's pl _ _?'
But Nim just slept the day away

Ardy was sad that Nim was a _ l_ _ p
He got so mad, he started to weep.

Then Ardy said, 'Wait, I don't have to feel blue
I will play by myself. That's what I'll will d _ !

Syllables

A syllable is a word or part of a word with a vowel sound formed by the opening and closing of the mouth.

The number of the vowel sounds heard in a word will determine the number of syllables the word will have.

Pebbles has a list of words. Let's find how many syllables are there in each word.

gar-den

bas-ket

muf-fin

drag-on-fly

pen-cil

horn

pear

rab-bit

Count the syllables in each word and then draw a line to matc with the right number.

cobweb	4
animal	1
lunch	2
caterpillar	3

Read aloud each word and write the syllables.

children ....

letter ....

movie ....

chicken ....

underground ....

banana ....

watermelon ....

monkey ....

chimpanzee ....

Look at the pictures and fill in the missing letters. Then, put a '-' to separate each syllable in the word.

_ l a _ t

t _ b _ e

_ i o _ i _

r a _ n b _ _

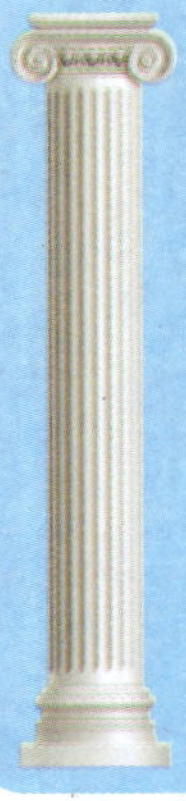

p _ _ l a _

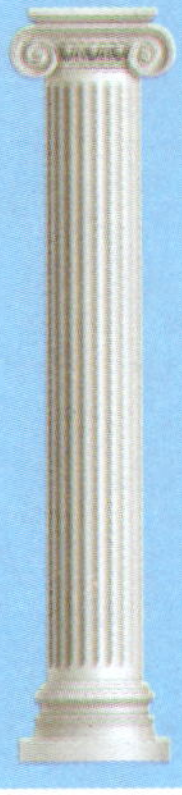

t _ _ d

f _ o w _ r

_ r a _ g _

Count and write the syllables in each word.

tuna .... ☐

seal .... ☐

fish .... ☐

octopus .... ☐

oyster .... ☐

whale .... ☐

dolphin .... ☐

shrimp .... ☐

crab .... ☐

starfish .... ☐

Compound Words

A compound word is formed when two words are combined to make a new word.

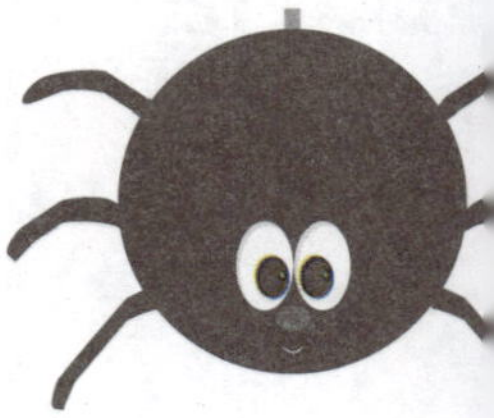

Spidy is here to give you a few examples of compound words.

sun + flower = sunflower	lady + bird = ladybird
star + fish = starfish	water + melon = watermelon
blue + berry = blueberry	butter + fly = butterfly
air + plane = airplane	paint + brush = paintbrush

Look at the pictures and write the new word for each pair.

....

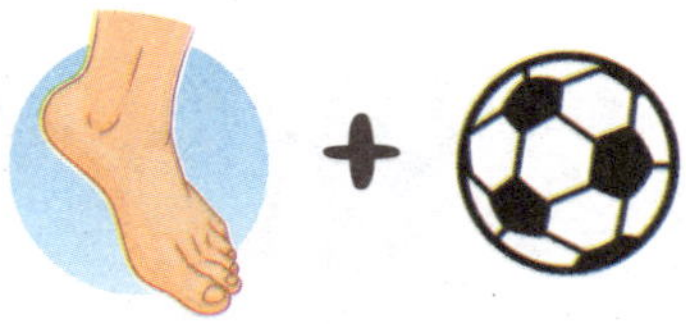

....

....

....

....

Draw a line between the two words to form a new word.
Chirpy is here to help you!

note	boat
book	paper
sub	berry
head	light
house	book
sand	shelf
straw	way
cow	mill
sun	glasses
wind	boy

Now, write the words here.

Help Molly with these word sums to make new words.

rattle
+ snake
....

arm
+ chair
....

cross
+ word
....

base
+ ball
....

rain
+ coat
....

pan
+ cake
....

ear
+ ring
....

skate
+ board
....

body
+ guard
....

lap
+ top
....

Identify and underline the compound word in the following sentences. Then help Dany the dog to write the words in the given space.

1. Mary and Sally are playing in the backyard.

.... = ... + ...

2. Rocky found a pencil near a riverbank.

.... = ... + ...

3. Nina eats a strawberry a day.

.... = ... + ...

4. Tom went to Italy in an airplane.

.... = ... + ...

5. Pam made a cake for breakfast.

.... = ... + ...

6. A butterfly has beautiful wings.

.... = ... + ...

7. The sails of the windmill were wheeling round.

.... = ... + ...

Singular and Plural

When nouns are singular, there is just one of them, such as orange. When the nouns are plural, there are more than one, such as nine lions. We usually create plural by adding 's' to the end. But if a word ends in s, ss, x, ch or sh we need to add 'es' to make it plural.

It is a rainy day and Froggy is sorting his things. Let's see what is he doing.

Froggy has left a few things. Could you help him put them in the right box?

cup, books, brushes, toy, shells, dresses, bat, balloons, necklace

Add **s** or **es** to the words to turn these into plurals.

feather + ... = ...

boy + ... = ...

animal + ... = ...

bus + ... = ...

zoo + ... = ...

match + ... = ...

house + ... = ...

panda + ... = ...

brush + ... = ...

carrot + ... = ...

mailbox + ... = ...

gas + ... = ...

Fill in the blanks with the plural form of the words in bracket. Add **s** or **es**.

1. There are seven .... (color) in the rainbow.

2. Travis ate a lot of .... (mango).

3. Kasey has pretty .... (dress).

4. Michaela has 4 beautiful .... (car).

5. Rick is five .... (year) old.

6. England has played two test ....(match) in the last series.

7. The forest is full of .... (tree).

8. She went to the party with her....................... (friend).

9. Don't take out the .... (crab) from the tank.

10. Two .... (fox) ran by the river.

Circle the singular words and underline the plurals in the box. Now, search the words in the given grid.

classes	candy	kittens	birds	kites
kids	balls	tulip	club	lunch

K	E	R	A	J	G	N	I	G	G	I	D
I	I	J	A	Y	P	D	V	C	L	I	N
T	U	D	H	T	U	L	I	P	T	O	O
E	T	V	S	T	T	V	Y	A	B	W	I
S	L	I	V	B	I	R	D	S	N	Q	S
E	U	H	E	U	E	L	A	S	R	D	N
V	N	C	N	O	I	O	S	E	E	Y	E
D	C	A	N	D	Y	B	L	S	V	N	T
A	H	A	S	K	U	M	L	S	O	A	T
I	Q	P	P	L	A	E	A	A	G	S	I
D	D	Y	C	S	J	N	B	L	P	T	K
E	U	H	E	R	I	T	A	C	E	Y	C

Color a star every time you find a word.

Spelling Quiz

1. Read the sentence aloud. Can you count and write the vowels and consonants in this sentence?

Aly is a cute girl.

Vowels: ....

Consonants: ....

2. Fill in the missing blends to complete each word and sentence.

a. Raja _ _ ives the car slowly.
b. Aliens travel in a _ _ aceship.
c. _ _ icks are used to make buildings.
d. Mike opened the wedding _ _ _ oll.

3. Match the rhyming pairs.

• class	• cat
• night	• floor
• bat	• flight
• door	• grass

4. Circle the correct plural word. Now, read aloud each word as you write.

a. foxs foxes ....
b. peaches peach ....
c. book books ....
d. dogs doges ....

Answers

Page 3: apple, ice cream, owl, eagle, octopus, abacus, egg, inkpot

Page 4: i, o, u, e, a, u

Page 5: angel,acorn; eagle,elf; island,ice; ocean,otter; under,uncle; insect,iron

Page 7: tissue, taxi, piano, menu, kiwi, mango, pizza

Page 8: a- idea,media,banana,pea; e- kettle,bottle; i- ski,litchi;
o- tomato,volcano,piano,video; u- emu,you,plateau

Page 9: taxi, globe, tornado, moustache, lava, tutu, ski

Page 11: log, bib, sun, cap, net, web, bin, fun

Page 12: sun, web, bin, man, tin, dog, cat, cap, log, toy

Page 13: dam, put, fox, leg, nib, bug

Page 14: toucan, panda, carrot, mango, tiger, sky, donkey, tomato, gorilla, spoon, love

Page 15: football, flower, dress, cherry, head, star

Page 16: zebra, pin, spoon, dam, panda, tent, mango, nest, bee, fish

Page 17: f,h; l,n; p,t; t,r; s,f

Page 19: glass, staff, dress, pizza, free, sleep, teeth, pull, muff, buzz

Page 21: glasses, shell, tall, tree, cuff, noon, grass, jazz, wool, muffin

Page 23: frog, bank, drink, brush, spoon, globe

Page 24: stork, snail, spider, grass, gloves, script, fruit, drum, brown

Page 25: long, spider, spotted, snake, gliding, grass, scream, stopped, frightened, friend, frog, snake

Page 26: tape, kite, robe, cube, hope, mate, pine, cute, note

Page 27: rat+e=rate; pan+e=pane; can+e=cane; man+e=mane; cap+e=cape

Page 28: tail, rain, day, snail, hay, vain; boil, oil, toy, enjoy, coin, noise

Page 29: writer, fry, prime, type, mild, gym, sink, dolphin, final; rhythm, ginger, pyramid, bicycle

Page 31: coat-boat, toad-road, tree-bee, sock-block, top-mop, feel-meal, blue-glue, pail-tail, dig-fig, rack-sack

Page 32: hot, house, boat, lock, sink, dish, cake, den, bell, van

Page 34: garden 2, basket 2, muffin 2, dragonfly 3, pencil 2, horn 1, pear 1, rabbit 2; cobweb 2, animal 3, lunch 1, caterpillar 4

Page 35: chil-dren, let-ter, mov-vie, chick-en, un-der-ground, ba-nan-a, wa-ter-mel-on, mon-key, chim-pan-zee

Page 36: plant, ta-ble, vi-o-lin, rain-bow, pil-lar, toad, flow-er, or-ange

Page 37: tu-na 2, seal 1, fish 1, oc-to-pus 3, oys-ter 2, whale 1, dol-phin 2, shrimp 1, crab 1, star-fish 2

Page 38: rainbow, football, cupcake, lighthouse, snowman

Page 39: notebook, bookshelf, subway, headlight, houseboat, sandpaper, strawberry, cowboy, sunglasses, windmill

Page 40: rattlesnake, armchair, crossword, baseball, raincoat, pancake, earring, skateboard, bodyguard, laptop

Page 41: backyard=back+yard, riverbank=river+bank, strawberry=straw+berry, airplane=air+plane, breakfast=break+fast, butterfly=butter+fly, windmill=wind+mill

Page 42: singular: cup, toy, bat, necklace; plural: books, brushes, shells, dresses, balloons

Page 43: feathers, boys, animals, buses, zoos, matches, houses, pandas, brushes, carrots, mailboxes, gases

Page 44: colors, mangoes, dresses, cars, years, matches, trees, friends, fishes, foxes

Page 46: vowels 4, consonants 8; drives, spaceship, bricks, scroll; class-grass, night-flight, bat-cat, door-floor; foxes, peaches, books, dogs